For Monica

Published by Modern Publishing
A Division of Unisystems, Inc.

Text and Illustration Copyright ©1989 by Martin Lemelman.
Copyright©1989 Modern Publishing, a division of Unisystems, Inc.

THE PARTY ANIMALS and character names are trademarks
of Martin Lemelman.

® Honey Bear Books is a trademark owned by Honey Bear
Productions, Inc., and is registered in the U.S Patent
and Trademark Office.

Printed in the U.S.A.

the PARTY ANIMALS COUNTDOWN TO FUN

Written and Illustrated
by Martin Lemelman

Modern Publishing
A Division of Unisystems, Inc.
New York, New York 10022

Why did Jake have such a great party?

Here are **10** terrific · reasons!

Beaky brought **10** beautiful balloons.

Jerry joyfully juggled 9 jellybeans.

Harry held 8 happy hats.

PARTY

8

Shelly saw 7 sparkling stars.

Sidney scooped 6 sweet sundaes.

6

Martin munched 4 marvelous marshmallows.

Terry tidied 3 terrific tables.

Paula picked 2 precious presents.

Crocket carried 1 carrot cake.

And Jake blew out all
1,2,3,4,5,6,7,8,9...10
candles!

The **PARTY ANIMALS** always have fun at their parties.

You can count on it!

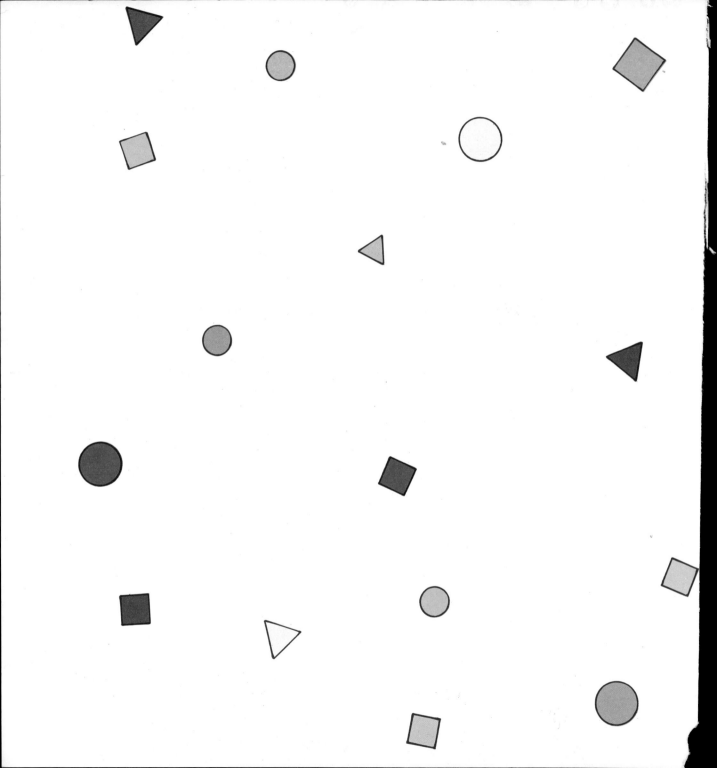